Tracks and Tales

Priya Rajendran

Copyright © 2025 by Priya Rajendran

All rights reserved.

This book or any portion there of may not be reproduced or used in any manner whatsoever without the express written permission of the respective writer of the respective content except for the use of brief quotations in a book review.

The writer of the respective work holds sole responsibility for the originality of the content and IndiePress is not responsible in any way whatsoever.

Printed in India

ISBN: 978-93-7197-070-9

First Printing, 2025

IndiePress

A division of Nasadiya Technologies Private Ltd.

Koramangala, Bengaluru

Karnataka-560029

http://indiepress.in/

Edited by MAP Systems, Bengaluru

Typeset by MAP Systems, Bengaluru

Book Cover designed by Sankhasubhro Nath

Publishing Consultant: Shrey Saboo

Contents

Preface vii
Acknowledgements ix
Author's Note xi
Foreword xiii

Kannadivalayal 1
The Saree 7
The First Love and The Last Bus 13
The Jet Man 19
Inja 25
The Journey Beyond 31
The Long Drive 35
The Stranger 39
The Endless Roads 43
The Unspoken Journey 47
The Waiting 51
A Love Left Behind 55
Whispers of the Night 65
Winds of Change 71
Lucky, But Not Lucky 77
The Last Splash 83

Glossary 91

Preface

Karma is the most powerful force in human existence. Gravity keeps us grounded, but it is the Law of Karma that separates humans from other species.

Life is a journey, often experienced through the roads we take, the tracks we cross, and the paths we dare to follow. Each story in this collection carries a unique flavour of these journeys—some physical, some emotional, and others spiritual. Tracks and Tales is a tapestry woven with the essence of human experiences, where every road leads to a story, and every track echoes with whispers of life's bittersweet moments.

These stories are not entirely new. In fact, they are inspired by the people we encounter in our day-to-day lives. Much like the comfort of a simple meal of curd rice and potato fry—a dish so regular yet so fulfilling—these stories hold a quiet familiarity. They reflect the ordinary moments that often carry extraordinary emotions, the small yet profound experiences that shape our lives in ways we may not immediately realise.

Every character, every journey in this collection, is drawn from the lives of people I've met during my travels. Their struggles, joys, hopes, and heartbreaks have stayed with me, compelling me to explore their perspectives and emotions. These are not tales of grandeur or spectacle, but stories of small, intimate moments—those fleeting emotions we all feel but rarely express.

Through this collection, I've tried to capture the essence of those human connections and perspectives, giving voice to the quiet, unspoken stories that exist all around us. You may find yourself feeling as though you've known these stories before—and perhaps that's the point. In their familiarity lies their power: the ability to resonate, comfort and remind us of the shared humanity that binds us all.

As you turn the pages of Tracks and Tales, I invite you to embark on these journeys with an open heart. May these stories evoke memories, spark emotions, and leave you with a sense of connection. After all, life itself is made up of these small, precious moments—and it is within their embrace that we find our greatest truths.

Thank you for choosing to travel with these tales. I hope you enjoy the ride.

Warm regards,
Priya Rajendran

Acknowledgements

First and foremost, I am deeply grateful to God for being my constant source of strength, hope, and guidance throughout this journey. Without his divine grace, none of this would have been possible.

To my mentor, **Director Cheran**, words cannot express my gratitude for your unwavering belief in me. You have been my guiding light, encouraging me to embrace my passion and trust in my abilities. Your faith in me has been a cornerstone of my journey, and I will forever cherish your support.

To my former manager, **Mrs Madhavi G**, who was more than just a supervisor—thank you for being a steady, mature presence during a defining phase of my life. When I was in my early 20s, just beginning to navigate adulthood, I often brought emotional confusion and immaturity into a corporate space. I showed tantrums, made impulsive choices, and struggled to differentiate passion from profession. At a time when many would have chosen to distance themselves or give up on me, you instead chose to guide me with patience, empathy, and wisdom. You once said, *"Vishnu, you are like a butterfly—I should let you fly* *rather than hold you down."* That line stayed with me. If not for your understanding and gentle mentorship, I could have been truly misguided. You helped me find my wings, and for that, I will always be grateful.

To my husband, **Mr Karthikeyan**, my partner in every sense of the word—you are my greatest supporter and my truest cheerleader. Thank you for helping me turn every dream into reality, for standing by me through every step, and for believing in me when I doubted myself.

To my father, **Mr Rajendran**, and my sister, **Mrs Gayathri Nikhil**, thank you for letting me be unapologetically myself. Your unconditional love and encouragement have given me the freedom to dream big and pursue my passions without hesitation.

To my family, I am deeply grateful for your unwavering support, unconditional love, and constant encouragement. You have all been my rock, my inspiration, and my source of comfort. This book is as much a reflection of your belief in me as it is of my journey.

This storybook exists because of you all. Thank you for being my foundation, my inspiration, my strength.

Author's Note

From the bustling corporate corridors of an HR professional to the creative chaos of an aspiring filmmaker, my journey has been anything but ordinary. Along the way, I discovered my love for travelling—a passion that has not only shaped my perspective on life but has also inspired the stories in this collection. Each story is like a small memory from my travels—a reflection of the people I've met, the emotions I've felt, and the moments I've cherished.

What I love most about these stories is their simplicity. They are not grand epics or dramatic tales, but glimpses into the lives of everyday people navigating their own worlds. They capture how often we find ourselves tied to the rules of society, cycling through routines, and missing the beauty in the ordinary. Through this collection, I hope to remind you of the magic in small moments and the unspoken stories that surround us everyday.

I've always believed that everyone has a story to tell, and this book is my way of sharing some of the stories I've encountered during my journey. I hope that, as you read these tales—perhaps during your own travels—you'll find them like a soothing melody, a companion to lighten your heart and ease your mind.

Thank you for picking up this book and allowing me to share these stories with you. It means the world to me.

Foreword

Whenever I see a writer's name, and it happens to be a woman's, I see it as a sign of progress. True freedom begins when women start recording what they really feel, in their own voice, and in the right way.

One such thoughtful woman I've had the pleasure of meeting is Priya Rajendran.

We talk a lot. We debate a lot. And one day, during one of those conversations, she casually mentioned, "I think I'm going to write stories."

I had no idea what she was capable of. I didn't know what direction her pen would take, what pages it would fill, whether it would paint the world in red or black or purple. But as a senior, I encouraged her—without expectations—purely because I believed in her fire.

Within a short span, she came back with sixteen stories, beautifully structured into a book. It surprised me. But once I started reading, the surprise turned into a quiet joy. Joy that came from the depth of thought behind her words.

A story can be fictional.

Or it can stem from a personal wound.

Or it can reflect the concern of a writer closely observing society.

But Priya stands apart.

She sketches characters inspired by the people around her, capturing the unspoken, deeply buried emotions that even those closest to these women might never notice. With sharp observation and poetic precision, she brings them alive.

She approaches women of different ages with maturity that evolves with their timelines—portraying not just as an author but as the voice of the character. It was refreshing to see that her portrayals weren't driven by a writer's personal desire but by an honest need to express the truth of the character's soul.

There is no force-fed imagination here. Even if the stories describe things hard to accept, they do so with grace—mirroring the quiet tragedies lived by many women.

Some emotions feel like dry leaves...

Some like tender shoots, freshly plucked...

And in some places, you feel as if the whole root has been pulled from the ground...

Amutha in Kannadi Valayal (The Glass Bangles),

Meenakshi whose heart burns within the burnt saree,

Irfan's love that gave Ananya wings at an airport goodbye,

The story Inja, where love defies age and tradition...

The grandmother and grandson who go on a long drive...

Wow.

As you read, you'll find many such tender, searing emotions across these sixteen stories.

And somewhere, you might find yourself remembering someone—maybe even yourself.

These sixteen stories also map the emotional journey of the writer herself.

Whether it's a poet, a painter, a writer, or a reformer—when someone learns to view an incident from many angles, their creation gains a powerful momentum. It draws us deep into the lives of people we've never met. And even if we've never lived those lives, the writer's grace lets us feel them.

A writer must speak. Through words. Through characters. Through their creations.

My heartfelt congratulations to the writer.

I'm eagerly waiting to see how many of her books will soon occupy the shelves of my personal library.

Let the intoxication of literature continue.

With warm wishes,
Cheran
Film Director/Writer

Kannadivalayal

It was late afternoon, and school had just ended, but Amutha returned home with a heavy heart. While other children rushed home with glee, chattering about their day, Amutha's situation was different. Growing up in the 1980s in Chennai, Tamil Nadu, in a conservative household, her life was shaped by her parents' deeply traditional mindset. Despite living in a bustling city with opportunities and exposure, Amutha's world was confined to the narrow boundaries of her family's beliefs. Her father, Gopinath, didn't necessarily believe that a girl's place was strictly within the home, but was convinced that the world outside was not safe for women. This belief fuelled his protective instincts, leading to strict rules that limited her freedom.

Her mother, though gentler in expression, supported her father's views, creating a home environment where caution often overshadowed exploration. Yet, within these restrictions, Amutha harboured a secret dream—a longing to explore the world beyond the bustling streets of Chennai, to feel the thrill of adventure she only read about in her school books.

When Amutha arrived home that day, she placed her schoolbag on a chair near the dining table and noticed a letter resting on it. Her heart leapt as she recognised the handwriting—it was from her aunt, announcing that she was coming to visit them next week.

Amutha's aunt was the only person in the family who had the freedom to explore life. She was never married and was always busy travelling. Whenever she was in town, Amutha had the rare chance to visit places with her. If not for her aunt, she would never have seen much beyond her neighbourhood. Her aunt's visits were the most exciting time of the year for Amutha.

The next week came, and Amutha was ready to welcome her aunt. As soon as she arrived, Amutha could hardly contain her excitement. That night at dinner, Amutha's father asked his sister about her plans. To Amutha's disappointment, she replied, 'This year, I have no plans. I just want to spend time with the children.'

Hearing that, Amutha's heart sank. She had been looking forward to an adventure, but now it seemed there would be none. She tried to hide her disappointment, but the weight of it lingered.

Two days later, as Amutha was helping her mother in the kitchen, her aunt suddenly rushed in, her face flushed with excitement.

'Where's Gopi?' she asked hurriedly.

'What happened, Anni?' Amutha's mother inquired, alarmed.

'There's been a change in my plans,' her aunt replied, catching her breath. 'I feel like I need to visit Mookambika. I met a few friends at the temple, and they were talking about the powers of Devi Mookambika. Now I can't get it out of my head—I feel drawn to visit her.'

Her enthusiasm set the wheels in motion. Plans were made swiftly, with everyone pitching in to organise the trip. Though Amutha loved the idea of travelling, she wasn't sure if she was ready for such a long journey. She murmured to her mother, 'Why can't Anni visit the Devi temple nearby? Aren't they both the same?'

Her mother scolded her sharply. 'Don't be over-smart! Just do as you're told.'

Early the next morning, the household bustled with activity as they prepared for the trip. Amutha dressed in her favourite frock, her nerves tinged with anticipation. The journey was both exciting and tiring, with the train rattling through endless landscapes. When they finally arrived, they checked into a modest motel nearby to freshen up.

Amutha wore the silk pattupaavadai and dhavani she had received for Deepavali that year. The shimmering fabric caught the light, and her aunt adored her, saying, 'You look beautiful, marumagaley.' Her words brought a shy smile to Amutha's face.

The temple premises were bustling with activity, packed with devotees. Her aunt, eager to ensure they had a smooth darshan, asked Amutha to wait near the shops while she checked for any special entry arrangements.

Amutha lingered near the rows of stalls, soaking in the vibrant atmosphere. Suddenly, a voice called out, 'Valayal, valayal, kannadi valayal!' Startled, she turned to see a young man, no older than 19 or 20, holding a tray of glass bangles.

He approached her hesitantly, his small moustache and neatly combed hair giving him an air of sincerity. 'Would you like to buy some bangles?' he asked, his voice soft but tinged with desperation.

Amutha glanced at the dusty bangles, her initial response a curt, 'I don't want them.'

Within seconds, his eyes welled with tears. 'My mother passed away,' he said quietly. 'I have to sell these bangles to feed my brother and myself.'

Something about his words struck a chord. There was a truth in his tone that she couldn't ignore. Moved, she opened her purse and pulled out a `100 note—the money her father had given her for the entire trip. She handed it to him.

The young man's eyes widened in shock. 'Madam, I don't have change for such a large amount,' he stammered.

'Keep it,' Amutha said firmly.

He looked at her in disbelief, gratitude shining through his sorrow. 'I've come to this temple so many times, but today, I feel like I've had the darshan of the Devi herself,' he murmured.

Before Amutha could respond, her aunt returned, her face clouded with irritation. 'Can't you wait? Why are you wasting time shopping before darshan?' she snapped, dragging Amutha toward the temple.

The young man called after her, 'Madam, please wait!' He handed her a dozen bangles before she was pulled away.

Even after returning to Chennai, Amutha couldn't shake the memory of his face. His deep eyes haunted her dreams, his voice lingered in her thoughts. She longed to see him again, but how? The opportunity seemed impossible—until she overheard her aunt speaking to her parents.

'I think we should make this an annual trip,' her aunt said. 'Devi Mookambika has been calling me, and I want to visit her every year.'

A spark of hope ignited in Amutha's heart. Maybe, just maybe, she would see him again next year.

The following year, her aunt didn't return as planned. Amutha's hope waned. Then, unexpectedly, after one and a half years, her aunt announced another pilgrimage. Though she had little faith left, she couldn't help but search for him. And finally, near the flower stalls, she saw him.

Their gazes met. The world faded away.

When darshan was over, she went to collect her sandals. He came beside her, leaned in, and whispered, 'I will be waiting.'

As she climbed into the bus, she looked out the window. His figure blurred as she closed her eyes, his face filling her vision.

'Amma, Amma!'

She opened her eyes. A beautiful young girl stood beside her, smiling.

'Tell me,' the girl asked, 'when was the last time you visited Mookambika temple?'

Amutha's fingers traced the glass bangles on her wrist. She looked out of the window and, with a wistful smile, said, 'Maybe 23 years ago, before my marriage.'

The forgotten, long-gone memory of him flashed through her mind for just a second.

The Saree

In the late 1980s, the winding roads of Tamil Nadu carried countless stories, woven into the lives of travellers. Among them was Meenakshi, a health nurse from the Tiruvannamalai district. Originally from Theni, she was a woman of quiet strength, deeply attached to her roots. Each time she managed to get a day off, she would eagerly return home, yearning for the comfort of her mother's cooking and the comfort of familiar walls.

This journey, however, was different. It was her first time travelling alone after her marriage. Instead of heading to her mother's home, a place of rest and care, she was travelling to her in-laws' house, where responsibilities awaited. Her new life weighed heavily on her. Meenakshi had always been her mother's little girl, learning to cook by her side, listening to her soothing voice reciting bedtime tales. Now, she carried the weight of expectations in a new household where love felt transactional, measured by fulfilled duties and maintained appearances.

That morning, she had carefully chosen her attire—a saree that held her mother's memory. It was not just a piece of clothing. Her mother had gifted it to her on the day she got her first salary, saying, 'Wear this when you feel lonely, ma. It will remind you that I'm always with you.' The saree, with its deep green fabric adorned with golden motifs, was more than just an outfit. Its softness reminded Meenakshi of the many nights she had fallen asleep in her mother's lap, the pallu draped over her like a warm blanket. Wearing it made her feel protected, even amid the chaos of the outside world.

The bus stand at Tiruvannamalai was bustling with life that morning. Hawkers shouted, advertising fresh peanuts and chai, while passengers jostled for seats. Meenakshi clutched her bag tightly, the saree's pallu carefully folded over her shoulder. She boarded the crowded bus and found a window seat, thankful for the brief respite from the noise.

Outside, the sun blazed mercilessly, with beads of sweat clinging to her forehead. As the bus lumbered forward, she leaned against the window, letting the hot wind dry her damp skin.

The journey stretched on, the uneven roads amplifying every bump and jolt. Around her, passengers engaged in lively conversations, their voices blending with the rhythmic hum of the engine. A young mother beside her struggled to calm a wailing child, while an elderly man in the front row recited prayers under his breath. Meenakshi observed them all, her thoughts oscillating between the life she had left behind and the one she was stepping into.

Her mind wandered to her childhood home in Theni, a quaint house encircled by lush green fields. She could almost smell the aroma of her mother's tamarind rice wafting through the kitchen, and hear her father's hearty laughter upon returning from the fields. In contrast, her new home felt distant and cold. Her in-laws were polite but formal, and Sundaram, her husband, was a man of few words. Though he cared for her in his own quiet way, Meenakshi often felt like a guest in her own life, unsure of where she truly belonged.

The bus stopped at a small village en route, and vendors swarmed the windows, selling everything from boiled groundnuts to colourful plastic trinkets. Meenakshi bought a paper packet of roasted peanuts, more from habit than hunger, and shared them with the little boy sitting beside her. His wide-eyed smile warmed her heart, momentarily easing her anxiety.

Hours later, the bus pulled into the bustling Madurai bus stand. The chaos was overwhelming—hawkers shouted, buses honked, and travellers hurried in every direction. Meenakshi stepped off with relief, stretching her cramped legs. She adjusted her saree absently, and that was when she noticed it. Her cherished saree, a symbol of her mother's love, bore cigarette burns on its pallu. The once-pristine fabric was now marred with blackened holes.

Her breath caught in her throat as she stared at the damage. A wave of emotions surged through her—anger, sadness, and helplessness. The saree had been her anchor, a thread connecting her to her mother's love and warmth. Now, it was tarnished, a painful reminder of how fragile even the most treasured things could be in the face of the world's carelessness.

She looked around, trying to identify the culprit, but the crowd was too dense, too indifferent. People brushed past her, each absorbed in their own struggles, oblivious to her silent anguish. Tears stung the corners of her eyes, but she blinked them away, swallowing her pain. She was a middle-class woman with a family to care for and no time to dwell on such incidents. Gathering the torn pallu, she boarded the next bus, her mind heavy with loss.

The journey to her in-laws' village felt endless. As the bus jolted forward, Meenakshi stared out of the window, watching the landscape blend into shades of green and brown. Her thoughts wandered back to her mother—the soft touch of her hands, the gentle words of wisdom she shared, and the way she used to drape this very saree over Meenakshi's shoulders. The burns seemed to tarnish not only the saree but also the precious memories tied to it.

A sense of vulnerability enveloped her. Would life always be this way? A cycle of compromises, losses, and silent battles? Yet, amid the despair, a spark of resilience began to flicker within her. She realised that the saree's damage, though heartbreaking, didn't erase the love it represented. Her mother's essence wasn't confined to the fabric; it lived on in the values she had instilled in Meenakshi, in the strength she had nurtured within her.

By the time Meenakshi arrived at her destination, she had composed herself. She stepped off the bus, ready to take on the roles expected of her. Her in-laws greeted her warmly, their smiles veiling unspoken expectations. She managed a polite smile in return, slipping seamlessly into the rhythm of her new life.

That night, as she folded the saree and placed it in her trunk, Meenakshi allowed herself a moment of quiet reflection. The burns on the pallu would remain, a permanent scar on something once beautiful. But they would also serve as a reminder—a testament to her resilience, her strength to endure and forward.

The world might be indifferent, even cruel, but Meenakshi knew she carried her mother's love within her. It wasn't in the saree alone; it was in every act of kindness she showed, every challenge she faced with silent courage. And that realisation, more than anything, gave her the strength to face whatever lay ahead.

The First Love and The Last Bus

In the small, quiet village of Alangudi, nestled in the heart of Pudukottai district, life moved with a predictable rhythm. Days were marked by the sound of roosters at dawn and the steady hum of cycles passing through narrow roads. Ranjith, a young man in his early twenties, had just completed his graduation. While his peers secured jobs or settled into family businesses, Ranjith lingered at home, weighed down by unmet expectations.

His father, a stern farmer, never hesitated to express his disappointment. 'What use is your education if it doesn't feed the family?' he would say, his voice tinged with frustration. These words, though often repeated, cut deep into Ranjith's soul. The household, already strained by his father's declining health, was further clouded by tension. His mother, caught between her husband's worries and her son's frustrations, tried her best to maintain peace.

In the midst of this turmoil, there was one solace in Ranjith's life—Subha. A girl from the same village, Subha was a vision of simplicity and grace. Her laughter was like the gentle rustling of leaves, a sound that lingered with Ranjith long after she left. They had grown up together, their paths crossing often, though always with an air of innocent awkwardness. Over time, his admiration for her blossomed into a quiet love. Yet, life's hardships made it difficult for him to focus on this affection, leaving his feelings unspoken.

One evening, a heated argument broke out between Ranjith and his father. The older man, weakened by illness, berated his son for his perceived irresponsibility. 'You've done nothing but waste your time!' he shouted. Ranjith, overwhelmed by anger and guilt, stormed out of the house. 'I'll return only when I've made something of myself!' he declared, his voice trembling with a mix of determination and despair.

Without a clear plan, Ranjith left Alangudi that night, boarding a bus to Pudukottai. The journey felt like an escape, the darkness outside mirrored his tumultuous emotions. As the bus rattled along, he vowed to prove his worth, to return with the means to support his family and silence his father's criticisms.

The days turned into months, and years. Ranjith moved from one odd job to the next, moving between towns and cities. The life he envisioned seemed always just out of reach. The constant struggle to make ends meet consumed him, and the memories of Alangudi faded away. Subha, once a beacon of hope in his life, became a distant memory, her laughter merely a faint echo in his memory.

Back in Alangudi, Subha's life took a different turn. Heartbroken by Ranjith's sudden departure, she struggled to understand why he had left without a word. Her parents, concerned for her future, arranged a marriage with a man from a neighbouring village. Subha entered the union with a heavy heart, her dreams of love and companionship dimmed by the weight of her reality.

Her husband, initially kind, soon showed his darker side. A chronic drinker and gambler, he squandered the family's modest earnings, plunging them into debt. Subha, now a mother, bore the brunt of his reckless behaviour, struggling to support her child amidst a loveless marriage. Her once-bright eyes grew weary, her laughter replaced by quiet sighs.

Years later, Ranjith received a telegram that would change everything. The message was simple but urgent: Mother unwell. Return immediately. The words jolted him out of his routine, stirred a sense of duty he had long buried. He packed his belongings and boarded the first train to Pudukottai, his heart heavy with guilt and anticipation.

The journey was long, and as the train chugged toward Pudukottai, memories of his village flooded back. He thought of his mother's gentle voice, his father's stern gaze, and Subha's radiant smile. By the time the train pulled into the station, the weight of his past pressed heavily on his chest.

Ranjith hurried to catch the last bus to Alangudi. The bus was almost empty, its dim interior filled with the faint hum of the engine. As the bus meandered through the dark countryside, Ranjith's mind wandered. He wondered how his parents would receive him after all these years. Would they welcome him with open arms or scold him for his long absence? And what of Subha? Had she moved on, as he had tried to?

At one of the stops, Ranjith's thoughts were interrupted by a flicker of movement outside the window. Another bus, heading in the opposite direction, had pulled up nearby. Through the dim light, he saw her—Subha. She was stepping off the bus, cradling a small child on her hip, her husband walking beside her. Her face, though older and wearier, still held the quiet beauty he remembered.

Ranjith's heart ached as he watched her, his mind racing with unspoken words. He wanted to call out to her, to bridge the gap that years and circumstances had created. But his voice faltered, and the moment slipped away. Subha, unaware of his presence, adjusted her child's shawl and vanished into the shadows with her husband.

The bus jolted forward, taking Ranjith further from the past he had momentarily seen. His heart felt heavy with regret, yet carried a strange sense of closure. Subha's presence, though fleeting, reminded him of the life he had left behind, the choices he had made, and the person he had become.

When the bus finally reached Alangudi, the familiar sights of his village greeted him. The fields, the narrow lanes, and the humble homes were just as he had left them. Yet, everything felt different. As he approached his house, he saw the flicker of a lantern in the window. His mother's frail figure appeared, her face brightening with a mixture of surprise and relief.

Ranjith stepped inside, the warmth of his home enveloping him. For the first time in years, he felt a sense of belonging. Yet, in the quiet corners of his heart, he knew he would forever carry the memory of Subha—the girl he had loved and lost, the one whose life had diverged from his in ways neither of them could have foreseen.

As the night deepened, Ranjith sat by the window, staring at the darkened road. The bus ride home had been more than a journey; it had been a passage through time, a confrontation with his past, and a reminder of the fleeting nature of love and life. The first love and the last bus—both had left their mark on his soul, moulding the man he was and the man he wished to become.

The Jet Man

The dense December fog hung heavily in the air, shrouding the narrow roads of Punjab. Ananya gripped the steering wheel tightly, her knuckles white with tension. The headlights of her rented car barely pierced through the mist, making every turn feel like a gamble. The scenic road trip she had taken to Shimla a week ago felt like a distant memory, overtaken by the stress of her current predicament. She was late—very late. Her flight from Delhi to Bangalore was scheduled for early morning, and now she was stranded far from the capital, unsure if she'd make it.

Her plan was simple: wake up early, drive back to Delhi, and board her flight. But oversleeping had thrown everything off course. By the time she reached the Delhi airport, the terminal was a chaotic sea of people, and the check-in queues stretched endlessly. Panic clawed at her chest as she joined the line, fumbling with her papers, her mind racing for solutions.

That's when she noticed him.

He stood a few feet behind her, tall and broad-shouldered, his posture radiating a calm confidence. His brown eyes, sharp and observant, caught the light, making them listen, and his well-kept beard added a rugged charm to his already striking features. People glanced his way, drawn to the effortless aura he carried. Ananya couldn't help but notice how he seemed to command attention without even trying.

'Need some help?' His deep voice broke through the noise around her— steady and reassuring.

Ananya turned to face him, her breath hitching slightly. She wasn't used to being noticed, especially in moments of distress. She nodded hesitantly, her voice barely audible. 'Yes, please,' she whispered, her flustered state causing her words to tremble.

The man offered a kind smile, his eyes softening. 'Let me talk to them,' he said, gesturing toward the airline staff. In minutes, he had sorted out the issue, his composed attitude cutting through the chaos like a knife. When he returned, ticket in hand, Ananya felt an overwhelming sense of relief.

'Thank you so much,' she said, her voice steadier now but still tinged with gratitude.

'Not a problem,' he replied. 'I'm Irfan.'

'Ananya,' she introduced herself, feeling an odd sense of connection to this stranger who had stepped in to help her without hesitation.

Little did she know, Irfan had a plan—one that had involved her from the moment he realised she was from Kerala. He needed someone local to blend in with while he carried out a hidden agenda there. But as he spoke to her, something shifted. The universe seemed to have other plans for him—plans he couldn't have foreseen.

They boarded the flight together, though their seats were apart. Yet, Ananya found herself glancing in his direction more than once. Irfan, seated two rows ahead, seemed impossible to ignore. His quiet intensity and commanding presence made him stand out, even in the crowded cabin. She wasn't the only one noticing him; whispers and stolen glances from other passengers confirmed that his magnetism was universal.

When the flight landed in Bangalore, both Ananya and Irfan discovered they had connecting flights to Kochi. In the bustling terminal, their paths crossed again, and this time, conversation flowed more naturally. Ananya, normally reserved and soft-spoken, found herself opening up to him in ways she hadn't anticipated. There was something about Irfan's Aura—his mix of confidence and approachability—that made her feel at ease.

Over the next few days, their interaction moved beyond the fleeting moments at the airport. Irfan reached out to her on Instagram, and what began as light exchanges quickly evolved into deep, late-night conversations. Ananya, unaware of Irfan's original intentions, found herself drawn to him. He had a way of making her feel seen, valued, and protected—a stark contrast to the loneliness she often felt in her own life.

But for Irfan, things weren't so simple. The more time he spent talking to Ananya, the harder it became to follow through with his plan. She wasn't just another face in the crowd; her kindness, innocence, and vulnerability struck a chord within him. He found himself questioning his actions, his choices, and the path he had been on for so long. Ananya had unknowingly become his anchor, pulling him back from the edge of darkness.

One evening, Irfan asked Ananya to meet him in Kochi. She agreed, assuming it was just a friendly gesture. What she didn't expect was for him to drive over 350 kilometres from Bangalore to see her that same evening. The gesture overwhelmed her, and as they drove along the scenic coastal roads, something shifted between them. Their connection deepened, no longer confined to fleeting conversations or shared glances. For the first time in years, Ananya felt genuinely cared for.

Irfan's feelings, too, had changed. He hadn't intended to fall for her, but he couldn't deny the pull she had on him. She made him want to be better, to leave behind the shadows of his past. But his life wasn't as simple as hers, and the weight of his secrets loomed over him.

One night, during one of their many late-night calls, Ananya shared with Irfan about her mother. 'I miss her smell,' she said softly, her voice trembling with emotion. 'She passed away when I was young, and sometimes I just wish I could feel close to her again. All I have is her sari, but it's not the same.'

Irfan listened intently, his heart aching for her. He asked her to send him the sari, though he didn't explain why. Trusting him completely, Ananya agreed, mailing the treasured garment to him without question.

Weeks later, Irfan called her to meet him one last time in Bangalore. When she arrived, he handed her a small, elegantly wrapped box. Inside was a perfume bottle. Confused, Ananya sprayed a little on her wrist and immediately tears welled up in her eyes. It was the scent of her mother, recreated perfectly.

'How did you...?' she began, her voice choked with emotion.

'I just wanted to give you something that would always remind you of her,' Irfan said softly. 'You deserve to hold on to her memory.'

Ananya hugged him tightly, overwhelmed by gratitude and love. But as she looked into his eyes, she saw a sadness she couldn't quite understand. Before she could ask, he kissed her forehead and whispered, 'Goodbye, Ananya.' And then he was gone.

Days turned into weeks, and Irfan's absence gnawed at Ananya. One evening, while strolling through the news, a headline caught her eye. The man she had fallen for was connected to activities much darker than she could imagine. Her heart shattered, the revelation tearing through her like a storm.

Yet, as she held the perfume bottle in her hands, she realised that Irfan had changed—for her, if only briefly. To her, he would always be Irfan—the man capable of only love. But the question haunted her—how could a man with so much love also be cruel? What made a person like him exist in two extremes? Love and darkness, tenderness and cruelty—bound within the same soul.

That question lingered in her mind, unanswered, like a whisper carried by the wind. And perhaps, she thought, some mysteries were never meant to be solved.

Inja

In the bustling city of Madurai, where politics was interwoven with everyday life, Mathivathani grew up with a passion for change. Raised by a grandfather who instilled in her the stories of revolutionaries and visionaries, she was captivated by stories of justice and equality. Among these stories, one figure stood out—Anbazhagan, a seasoned politician whose speeches electrified the masses and whose actions championed the values of integrity and fairness.

Within the confines of her conservative household, Mathivathani followed Anbazhagan's journey with reverence. She collected newspaper articles about him, memorised his speeches, and devoured every book he authored. While her peers admired movie stars, Mathivathani's idol was this man who fought for justice with unwavering resolve. What began as admiration slowly transformed into a deeper connection—an unspoken love for the ideals and humanity he embodied.

As years passed, Mathivathani's life began to align with her aspirations. After completing her degree in social work, she joined Anbazhagan's political party, determined to contribute to the causes she believed in. Initially, she was just another volunteer, working diligently behind the scenes. But her dedication and intelligence soon caught the attention of senior leaders. It wasn't long before Anbazhagan himself noticed her contributions, her sharp mind, and the passion that distinguished her.

Their first meeting was brief but impactful. Mathivathani had prepared meticulously for a presentation on a women's welfare scheme. Anbazhagan listened attentively, nodding approvingly as she outlined her proposal. At the end of her presentation, he looked at her with a rare smile. 'Well done,' he said simply. For Mathivathani, those simple words were monumental, a validation of everything she had worked toward.

As the months went by, Mathivathani became a trusted member of the party's social initiatives. She worked closely with Anbazhagan on various campaigns, often staying late to ensure every detail was perfect. Her admiration for him deepened as she witnessed his unwavering commitment to his constituents. But as their professional relationship grew, so did her personal feelings for him. She began to notice the little things—the way his eyes softened when he spoke about the underprivileged, the subtle lines of weariness on his face after a long day, and the kindness that lay beneath his formidable exterior.

Anbazhagan, though initially oblivious to her affection, couldn't ignore the sincerity in Mathivathani's actions. Her presence became a source of comfort amidst the chaos of his demanding life. Despite the vast age difference and the potential complications, he found himself drawn to her honesty and dedication. Their connection grew stronger, unspoken yet undeniable.

One evening, fate intervened in a way neither of them could have anticipated. Anbazhagan's driver was delayed, and he was running late for a crucial meeting. Mathivathani, who was nearby, offered to drive him. He hesitated before finally agreeing. The drive through the quiet streets of Madurai became a turning point. As they navigated the city, their conversation flowed effortlessly, covering topics ranging from politics to philosophy. For the first time in years, Anbazhagan felt a sense of ease, a reprieve from the constant scrutiny of public life.

This simple act of kindness marked the beginning of a bond that transcended professional boundaries. Late-night drives became their sanctuary—a space where they could shed their roles and be their true selves. For Mathivathani, these moments were everything she had dreamed of a chance to be close to the man she had loved from afar. For Anbazhagan, they were a rare respite, a reminder of the humanity he often sacrificed for his public duties.

But as their closeness grew, so did the challenges. Anbazhagan was acutely aware of the risks—the age difference, the potential for scandal, and the power dynamics at play. He questioned whether Mathivathani's feelings were genuine love or the idealisation of a young woman for a powerful man. Yet, despite his reservations, he found it increasingly difficult to maintain a distance. The sincerity in her eyes, the unwavering support she offered, broke down the walls he had built around his heart.

One evening, while they were waiting at a traffic signal, Mathivathani was deeply engrossed in conversation, her enthusiasm lighting up the car. She didn't notice that the light had turned green, nor did she see the impatient honking behind them. Anbazhagan, with a fond smile, simply said, 'Signal pottachu, Inja,' meaning 'The signal is on, let's go.'

The word slipped out naturally, as though it had always belonged between them. Mathivathani's breath hitched, her heart swelling with emotions too complex to name. It was at that moment she knew—he saw her, truly saw her. Not just as a dedicated worker or a follower, but as someone who had nestled herself into his heart.

As their relationship deepened, Mathivathani threw herself further into her work, often at the expense of her health. Her parents grew increasingly concerned, urging her to take care of herself, but she dismissed their worries. Her focus was solely on supporting Anbazhagan and his causes. But her relentless dedication took its toll. Persistent coughs and fatigue gave way to a more serious illness. One day, she collapsed during a meeting and was rushed to hospital, where she was diagnosed with pneumonia aggravated by a long-ignored lung infection.

When Anbazhagan heard of her hospitalisation, his world came crashing down. Despite the risks to his reputation, he rushed to the hospital. As he entered her room, seeing Mathivathani—frail, pale, and connected to machines—broke his heart. She asked everyone to leave, wanting to spend her final moments alone with the man she had loved so deeply.

Tears filled Anbazhagan's eyes as he sat by her bedside. He scolded her gently for neglecting her health and for sacrificing so much for his cause. But Mathivathani, with a weak smile, reassured him that she had no regrets. 'I lived my life loving you,' she said softly. 'And I always wished to leave this world before you— so I could die loving you, not mourning you.'

As her voice grew weaker, Mathivathani made one last request—a kiss on her forehead and to hear him call her 'Inja' one last time. Anbazhagan, his heart breaking, leaned down and kissed her gently. 'En Inja ippadi pesura,' he whispered, his voice trembling with emotion. A serene smile spread across Mathivathani's face as she closed her eyes, her soul at peace.

In the quiet that followed, Anbazhagan sat alone, holding her lifeless body of the woman who had loved him unconditionally. Though time passed, and he aged, the love Mathivathani had given him never faded. Even after years, he could still hear her voice, still feel her presence in the causes he fought for. Her love became his strength, a constant, unwavering force that kept him moving forward.

Though Mathivathani was gone, her spirit lived on in every decision Anbazhagan made, in every battle he fought. She left an indelible mark on his life, her love a reminder of the beauty and fragility of human connections.

The Journey Beyond

The train rattled along the tracks, the rhythmic clatter of wheels on steel filling the air as it wound its way through the countryside. Inside the coach, passengers settled into their seats, some dozing off, others lost in thought, and a few engaged in quiet conversations. Among them was an elderly woman, seated alone near the window. Her name was Lakshmi, a retired government employee in her early 60s, her life was a tapestry of responsibilities and obligations.

Lakshmi was always a woman of routine. Her days were once filled with the structured rhythm of work—files to be processed, meetings to attend, papers to sign. But now, after years of service, she retired, her time now supposedly her own. Yet, in reality, her life was still dictated by the needs and demands of those around her.

Earlier that day, her daughter, son-in-law, and grandson had accompanied her to the Coimbatore station. The little boy had clung to her leg, tears streaming down his face as he pleaded with her not to leave. Lakshmi's heart ached as she comforted him, knowing that she would miss his innocent laughter, his endless questions, and the way he made her feel needed.

Her daughter had fussed over her, making sure she was settled in her seat, her tiffin box safely tucked away in her bag. 'Amma, call me if you need anything,' her daughter had said, her voice laced with concern. 'And don't forget to eat the snacks I packed for you.'

As the train pulled away from the station, Lakshmi's phone rang, the screen lighting up with her daughter's name. She answered, placing the phone on speaker to combat the noise of the train.

'Amma, you left your tiffin box in a hurry,' her daughter's voice crackled through the phone.

'I have it with me,' Lakshmi replied, glancing at the bag beside her.

After a while, Lakshmi felt a pang of hunger and called her daughter again. 'I'm feeling hungry,' she admitted.

'There are snacks in the bag, Amma. Have some. And don't worry about the little one. He's fine now,' her daughter reassured her.

Soon after, her son-in-law's voice came over the line. 'Aunty, don't worry too much. You shouldn't encourage him when he cries like that. It's better if he learns not to associate your visits with you leaving.'

'Yes, yes, I understand,' Lakshmi said, though her heart still ached at the memory of her grandson's tears.

She ended the call and stared out the window, watching the landscape rush by. The phone rang again—this time it was her husband. They exchanged the usual pleasantries, discussing the events of the day, the small details of life that filled the gaps in their conversation. Her husband, in his usual gentle manner, reminded her to take care of herself and not to worry too much about their son-in-law's insistence on discipline.

As the train sped along, Lakshmi couldn't shake a growing sense of restlessness. She had always done what was expected of her—first as a daughter, then as a wife, and later as a mother. Now, even in her retirement, her life seemed to revolve around others. There was little room left for her own thoughts and desires.

A few stations later, two passengers took the seats beside her. They were middle-aged men, friendly and talkative. Lakshmi, feeling the need for distraction, engaged them in conversation. They discussed a wide range of topics—politics, nationalism, and even the stock market. The men were surprised and impressed by her knowledge and understanding.

'You know, I've never met someone your age who's so well-informed,' one of the men remarked, a note of admiration in his voice.

Lakshmi smiled modestly, but inside, something stirred. It had been so long since she had had an intellectual conversation, since she had spoken to someone who saw her as more than just a wife, mother, or grandmother. For a moment, she felt like the woman she had once been—sharp, independent, and curious about the world.

The conversation continued, the hours passed by unnoticed. As the train approached Chennai, the station where Lakshmi was supposed to disembark, a thought crossed her mind—what if she stayed on? What if, just this once, she let the train take her somewhere else, somewhere she hadn't planned to go?

The thought was both thrilling and terrifying. She had never done anything like this before. Her life was always about following rules and fulfilling duties. But now, as the train slowed down and the station came into view, Lakshmi felt a pull, a desire to keep moving forward, to see where the journey would take her.

She hesitated, her hand gripping the armrest. The men beside her noticed and asked if everything was all right.

'I'm fine,' she said, her voice steady, but her heart raced with the possibilities. The train came to a stop, and she saw the familiar sight of Chennai Central through the window—the bustling platform, the sea of people, the chaos of arrival. Instead of collecting her belongings and disembarking, Lakshmi stayed in her seat.

The train jolted forward, and with it, Lakshmi felt a shift within her. She didn't know where she was going, or what she would find, but for the first time in a long time, she felt free—free to make her own choices, to explore the world on her terms.

The men beside her continued talking, oblivious to the significance of her decision. But Lakshmi knew that in that moment, she had taken the first step on a journey that was hers alone.

As the train carried her further away from the life she had always known, Lakshmi leaned back and exhaled a breath she didn't know she was holding. The world outside was vast and unknown—but it was hers to explore.

The Long Drive

Manonmani was born and raised in the quiet embrace of a remote village nestled among rolling hills. The world she knew was simple, her days filled with the rhythm of farming, the soft rustling of paddy fields, and the chatter of her family. Yet, even as a child, she harboured dreams that reached far beyond the boundaries of her small village.

Her fascination began early, from the moment she learned in school that wheels were the first major development of civilisation. The idea that something so simple could lead to great journeys, discoveries, and progress fascinated her. She would run barefoot to the edge of the village whenever she heard the low rumble of a bus or the distant hum of a car engine. Standing by the roadside, she watched the vehicles pass, leaving trails of dust and whispers of distant places. To Manonmani, these vehicles were more than machines; they were magical, carrying people to destinations she could only imagine. The thrill of movement and the idea of exploring new places captivated her young heart.

'Where do these buses go, Appa?' she would ask her father, her eyes wide with curiosity.

'To the city, my dear,' he would reply with a gentle smile. 'A place bustling with people, lights, and endless roads.'

The city seemed like a faraway dream, a world too distant for a girl like her. But dreams, no matter how improbable, have a way of taking root. As Manonmani grew, her longing for travel deepened. She imagined herself in a brightly coloured bus, the wind in her hair, the road stretching endlessly ahead. While other girls in the village dreamed of marriage and family, Manonmani dreamed of journeys—of seeing the world beyond the hills that encircled her home.

However, life had other plans for her. Following the customs of her community, Manonmani was married young and soon became a mother. Her days became a cycle of responsibilities—cooking meals, tending to the household, and raising her children. The joy of nurturing her family filled her heart, but the quiet yearning for adventure never truly left her. She often stared wistfully at the road, wondering about the lives of those who travelled upon it.

Years passed, and Manonmani's children grew up and started families of their own. Though her life was busy with grandchildren and family gatherings, the fire within her to see the world remained unextinguished. Her family often teased her about her love for vehicles.

'Patti, why do you stare at the buses like that?' her youngest grandson, Ravi, would ask, laughing.

'Because they carry stories, my dear,' Manonmani would reply with a twinkle in her eye. 'Stories of people, places, and adventures.'

Her grandchildren adored her stories, but they didn't fully grasp the depth of her longing. To them, her fascination with

The Long Drive

travel was endearing but impractical. 'One day, Patti, we'll take you on the longest journey of your life!' Ravi would declare with enthusiasm. His promise always made her smile, even as she doubted it would ever come true.

One evening, as the family gathered on the veranda, Ravi sat beside Manonmani, his face lit with a mischievous grin. 'Patti, I have an idea. Let's go on a road trip! Just the two of us. We'll drive from the city to our village, stopping at all the places you've always wanted to see.'

Manonmani's heart raced with excitement. Was this finally happening? 'Really, Ravi? You'll take me?' she asked, her voice trembling with joy and disbelief.

'Yes, Patti,' Ravi assured her, taking her hands in his. 'You've spent your whole life dreaming of this. It's time to make it happen.'

The days before the trip were filled with anticipation. Manonmani spoke of the places she wanted to visit—temples, rivers, bustling markets—and Ravi listened patiently, making plans to fulfil her every wish. She couldn't contain her excitement, telling everyone in the village about her upcoming adventure. 'I'm finally going to see the world!' she declared, her eyes sparkling.

The night before the journey, Manonmani lay in bed, unable to sleep. Her mind brimmed with visions of the open road, wind in her hair, and laughter shared with Ravi. For the first time in years, she felt truly alive, as though the dreams she had held onto for so long were finally within her grasp.

But when morning came, Manonmani did not wake up. Sometime during the night, her heart—brimming with anticipation and happiness—had quietly stopped.. She passed away peacefully in her sleep, her lips curved in a faint smile.

The news of her passing reverberated through the family, leaving them in deep shock. Ravi was devastated, unable to reconcile the joy of their plans with the emptiness her absence created. He sat by her bedside, holding her hand, whispering apologies for the journey they would never take together.

On the day of her funeral, the family decided to fulfil a part of her dream in their own way. Her body was placed in an ambulance, and Ravi chose a route that mirrored the road trip they had planned. As the vehicle wound its way through the countryside, passing the places Manonmani had longed to see, her family followed in a solemn procession.

The journey was bittersweet. Each stop along the way—a temple, a riverside, a bustling market—felt like a tribute to the vibrant spirit of the woman who had always dreamed of seeing more. Ravi, driving behind the ambulance, imagined her smiling in the backseat, marvelling at the sights she longed to experience.

When they finally reached the village, the entire community gathered to pay their respects. They remembered Manonmani not just as a loving grandmother and a kind neighbour but as a dreamer whose heart was full of wanderlust.

In the days that followed, Ravi made a promise to himself. 'Patti may not have lived to see her dream come true, but I'll carry her spirit with me on every journey I take,' he said, gazing at the road that had once captivated her.

And so, Manonmani's legacy lived on—not just in the memories of her family but in every step Ravi took on her behalf. Her story served as a reminder that dreams, no matter how small or improbable, can inspire beyond a lifetime.

The Stranger

The sun had begun to dip below the horizon, colouring the misty hills of Ooty with shades of amber and pink. The winding road seemed to stretch endlessly ahead as Anjali gripped the steering wheel, with a grip that reflected the tension building inside her. This was her first time driving in the hills, and though her aunt continually praised her driving skills from the passenger seat, Anjali couldn't shake her apprehension. Her cousin sat in the backseat, scrolling through his phone, oblivious to the world outside.

Suddenly, a sharp thud jolted the car, jolting all three passengers forward. Anjali's heart raced as she instinctively hit the brakes and pulled over to the side of the road. Her breath caught in her throat as she realised what had happened—she had hit a bike.

Panic surged through her. 'Oh no, oh no, what have I done?' she gasped, fumbling to unbuckle her seatbelt.

Her aunt and cousin quickly scrambled out of the car, following Anjali to the scene. The bike lay sprawled on the road, its rider slowly rising to his feet. He dusted himself off, his helmet still on, and turned to face them. Anjali's voice trembled as she spoke, her words spilling out rapidly. 'Are you okay? I'm so sorry! I didn't see you—'

The man raised a hand to calm her. 'It's alright. I'm fine,' he said, his voice steady, almost soothing. He removed his helmet, revealing a kind face and a warm smile. 'The potholes here are impossible to avoid. I lost my balance—it's not your fault.'

Anjali's hands shook as she fumbled for her phone. 'Let me at least pay for the damage,' she insisted, her guilt overwhelming. She opened Google Pay, transferring an amount to him despite his protests. 'Please, I won't feel right if I don't.'

He finally relented, not wanting to prolong her distress. 'Thank you,' he said simply, pocketing his phone.

Anjali returned to the car, her heart still pounding. Her aunt and cousin reassured her that it wasn't her fault, but the incident lingered in her mind long after they drove away. What she didn't know was that this wasn't the first time the man had seen her.

His name was Aryan, and he had noticed Anjali before—on several occasions, in fact. The first time was at a traffic signal in Coimbatore. Aryan had been sitting on the back of his friend's bike, waiting for the light to turn green. In the car next to him was Anjali, completely absorbed in a game of Candy Crush on her phone. Her furrowed brow and the intense focus amused him. He found himself silently cheering for her to match the colours before the signal changed.

The second time was at a mall food court, where Anjali sat surrounded by her family, her laughter echoing through the space. Aryan, seated a few tables away, couldn't help but watch her. There was something about her—an unguarded joy, a simplicity that drew him in. He had admired her from afar, never imagining their paths would cross in such an unexpected way.

A week after the accident, Anjali received a message on Instagram from an unfamiliar account. The message read, 'Sometimes people meet accidentally... just like us.' She smiled at the clever wordplay and replied with a simple thank you.

From that day, Aryan began checking in on her occasionally. He wasn't intrusive, but whenever Anjali posted something thoughtful or melancholic, he would leave a kind word or a light-hearted joke to lift her spirits. Over time, she began to appreciate his quiet presence in her life. He was like a guardian angel, always present in the background, never requesting anything in return.

Months passed, and Aryan's occasional messages became a comforting constant. On her birthday, Anjali found herself scrolling through her Instagram inbox, hoping to see a message from him amidst the flood of well-wishes from friends and family. Sure enough, there it was: 'Happy Birthday, Anjali. I hope this year brings all things you deserve.' Touched by his thoughtfulness, she replied, 'Thank you, Aryan. It means a lot.'

As the days turned into weeks, Anjali couldn't deny the growing connection she felt toward Aryan. Though they had never met in person since the accident, he had become a part of her life in a way few others had. He was a steady source of positivity, someone she could count on even from a distance.

One evening, as she sat by her window watching the rain, Anjali made a decision. She wanted to meet Aryan, to thank him in person for being there for her. She sent him a message: 'Would you like to grab coffee sometime? I'd love to finally meet you.'

His response was almost immediate: 'Sure! But are you planning to hit me again? ;)'

Anjali laughed, her cheeks flushing with warmth. They agreed to meet the following weekend at a cozy café in the city.

The day of their meeting arrived, and Anjali found herself at the café early, her heart pounding with anticipation. She chose a table by the window, her eyes scanning every bike that passed by. But as the minutes turned into hours, Aryan didn't show.

She checked her phone repeatedly, hoping for a message explaining his delay, but there was nothing. The café began to empty as closing time approached, and Anjali finally left, disappointment weighing heavily on her heart.

For the next few days, she tried reaching out to him, but her messages went unanswered. She couldn't understand why he had disappeared so suddenly, leaving her with more questions than answers to hold onto.

What Anjali didn't know was that Aryan had lost his life while riding down to meet her. A reckless driver speeding out of control, had taken away a life built so carefully, a dream shattered in a split second.

His phone was never recovered, and the messages she sent were left unread, lost in the void of what could have been.

Anjali visited that café a few times after that, still hoping to see him, unaware that he had become something more—a presence that would forever linger in her life, a guardian angel watching over her. Life, she realised, was unpredictable. A single moment of carelessness, a fleeting second, could alter destinies. And though she never got to meet Aryan that evening, he remained a part of her story, a reminder that fate wove its own designs, beyond the grasp of human control.

The Endless Roads

Jothi grew up in Megamazhai, a remote village where time seemed to stand still. Days were punctuated by the hum of cicadas, the occasional roar of a passing bus, and the rhythm of life that never seemed to change. Her childhood was a blur of chores and hardships, marked by her father's volatile temper and the void left by her mother's absence. Her dreams, though, were vivid and full of hope. She longed for a life beyond the dusty roads and small houses of Megamazhai.

Raju, a young taxi driver, became her beacon of hope. He was a frequent visitor to the village, ferrying passengers to and from nearby towns. With his easy smile and kind behaviour, he was unlike any man Jothi had ever known. He spoke of Madurai, a bustling city of life and opportunity, and to Jothi, it seemed like paradise. Their encounters were brief yet meaningful—moments of laughter and shared dreams that made Jothi feel alive.

As their bond deepened, Raju began taking her on short trips to nearby destinations. Alagar Kovil, with its ancient temple nestled amidst greenery, became their sanctuary. The serene beauty of Kodaikanal offered a respite from the harsh realities of their lives, and the cascading waters of Suruli Falls seemed to echo Jothi's newfound optimism. Each trip was a step closer to her dream of escaping Megamazhai's confines.

Their decision to move to Madurai felt like a triumph. They rented a small room in a bustling neighbourhood, and for the first time, Jothi felt free. The city's vibrancy energised her, and every morning she woke up with a sense of purpose. She found work at a local supermarket, while Raju continued driving his taxi. Weekends were spent exploring temples, indulging in street food, and marvelling at the city's endless possibilities.

Jothi's happiness soared when she discovered she was pregnant. The news brought fresh hope into their lives. Raju, thrilled at the thought of becoming a father, promised her that their child would have a better life—a life free from the hardships they had endured.

The day their daughter was born, Jothi's world transformed. Holding the tiny, fragile life in her arms, she felt a deep sense of purpose. She vowed to protect her child from the cycles of pain that had defined her own childhood. For a while, it seemed like everything was falling into place.

But life in the city came with its own challenges. Raju's earnings from his taxi were inconsistent, and the pressure of supporting a family began to weigh on him. He found solace in a group of friends who promised to help him find better opportunities. At first, their camaraderie gave Raju hope. He often came home with stories of potential jobs and new ventures, and Jothi, though wary, trusted him.

However, the promises soon turned hollow. The friends who had seemed so supportive introduced Raju to the city's darker side. Casual drinking turned into nightly binges, and innocent games of cards escalated into high-stakes gambling. The man Jothi had once adored was slipping away, consumed by a world of vice and false promises.

Jothi tried everything to bring him back. She pleaded with him, reminded him of their dreams, and even accompanied him to deaddiction centres. But her efforts were met with resistance, and the man she had fallen in love with seemed further out of reach with each passing day.

The breaking point came one fateful night. Raju, in a drunken rage, lashed out and struck their daughter. The sight of her child crying in fear brought back painful memories of Jothi's own childhood. She remembered the nights spent cowering in the corner, terrified of her father's anger, and she knew she couldn't let her daughter suffer the same fate.

Summoning all her strength, Jothi confronted Raju. Her voice trembled, but her resolve was unwavering. 'I can't let our daughter grow up in fear,' she said, her eyes brimming with tears. 'If you can't change, you can't stay.'

Raju, defeated and ashamed, packed his belongings and left. As the door closed behind him, Jothi felt a mix of relief and sorrow. The dreams they had once shared were gone, replaced by the harsh reality of starting over on her own.

In their small room, Jothi cradled her daughter and reflected on her journey. She thought of her mother, who had walked away from a similar life, and she understood her mother's choices in a way she never had before. Jothi realised that many women like her tried to escape cycles of hardship, only to find themselves trapped in new ones. Breaking free wasn't easy, but she was determined to succeed—for herself and for her daughter.

The roads of Madurai no longer seemed filled with endless possibilities, but Jothi knew they were hers to navigate. She took on extra shifts at the supermarket, learning to manage her time and finances with precision. Slowly, she started to rebuild her life. Her days were long and tiring, but every step forward felt victorious.

On weekends, she took her daughter to the park, watching her play and laugh without a care in the world. Those moments reminded Jothi of why she was fighting so hard. She wasn't just building a life; she was creating a future free from the pain and fear that had haunted her past.

Jothi's journey wasn't easy, but it was hers. The roads she travelled were still winding and still uncertain, but they were no longer shaped by the dreams of others. She had found her strength in the face of adversity, and with each passing day, she became more determined to ensure her daughter would grow up knowing love, security, and the freedom to imagine.

The Unspoken Journey

It was the early 1990s, an era when train journeys were more than just transportation; they were a cultural experience, especially in South India. Families prepared meticulously for these trips, packing home-cooked meals, arranging blankets for the chilly nights, and providing entertainment for restless children. Delays were frequent, yet no one seemed to mind. For many, the journey was as important as the destination.

This particular journey began in Madurai, a bustling city teeming with history and life. The train, destined for the sacred town of Rameswaram, was a lifeline connecting the mainland to the island. Among the passengers was a group of young cousins, buzzing with the excitement of a long-anticipated pilgrimage. Their chatter filled the compartment as they settled into their seats, with bags and snacks scattered around them.

Amidst the boisterous group was Meena, the quiet one who often found herself lost in observation. As her cousins talked and laughed, Meena's gaze wandered across the compartment. It fell upon a pair of foreign tourists seated opposite her—two men with backpacks and guidebooks, their eyes scanning the scenery with a mixture of fascination and bewilderment.

One of the men caught her attention. He had light brown hair and a kind face, his features lit by the soft sunlight streaming through the window. Their eyes met briefly, and Meena quickly looked away, a shy smile tugging at her lips. She didn't know why, but something about him attracted her so much.

The train lurched forward, its whistle cutting through the hum of the station. As it gathered speed, the scenery outside transformed into lush fields and serene rivers. The cousins shared homemade snacks, giggling over inside jokes, but Meena's attention kept drifting back to the young man. She noticed how he tried to follow their Tamil conversation, his head tilting slightly in concentration. Despite the language barrier, his curiosity was clear.

Their interactions were silent yet profound: a stolen glance here, a tentative smile there. They communicated without words, the connection between them deepening with each passing mile. Meena found herself wondering about him—where he came from, why he was on this journey, and what stories he carried with him.

The rhythmic clatter of the train served as a backdrop for their silent bond. As the train crossed the iconic Pamban Bridge, with the turquoise sea stretching endlessly on either side, Meena stole another glance at the man. His eyes were wide with wonder, his camera clicking away to capture the breathtaking view. She smiled to herself, feeling a strange sense of pride in the beauty of her homeland.

The train pulled into Rameswaram, and the group of cousins disembarked with their belongings. The day unfolded in a flurry of temple visits, prayers, and exploration. The majestic corridors of the Ramanathaswamy Temple and the smell of incense filled the air, creating an atmosphere of reverence. Yet, amidst the spiritual grandeur, Meena's thoughts wandered to the young man from the train. She wondered whether he had found the town as enchanting as she did.

That evening, as they boarded the return train, Meena's heart skipped a beat. There he was, seated a few rows away, his expression lighting up in recognition. This time, their eyes met and lingered, and the faintest of smiles passed between them. She returned to her seat with her cousins, her heart racing in a way it never had before.

As the train made its way back to Madurai, the conversations around her became background noise. Meena's focus was on the young man, who occasionally glanced her way. Near the end of the trip, as the train neared the city, he stood up and approached her. Her cousins paused their chatter, watching curiously.

He held out a slip of paper with a number written on it—a coin phone number, common for public booths in those days. Meena hesitated, her heart pounding as she took the paper. He gestured to himself, mimed a phone call, and pointed at the paper, his meaning clear. She nodded shyly, her cheeks flushed with warmth.

As the train pulled into Madurai, they exchanged one last, lingering look before they parted ways. Meena tucked the paper into her bag, the weight of their unspoken connection filling her heart.

Years passed, and life moved on, but the memory of that brief encounter lingered. Meena often replayed the journey in her mind, her thoughts drifting back to the young man's kind eyes and warm smile. The slip of paper with the faded phone number became a cherished keepsake, a tangible reminder of their fleeting connection.

Every time she travelled to Rameswaram, Meena scanned the faces of passengers, hoping to see him again. But he was never there. She wondered where he was, if he thought of her, and what had become of his life.

Meena's own life took its course. She married a kind man from her village, raised a family and settled into the rhythms of domestic life. But even as she embraced her responsibilities, the memory of that train journey remained a quiet presence in her heart. In moments of solitude, she would retrieve the piece of paper from its hiding place, trace the faded numbers with her fingers, and allow herself to wonder about the paths they both had taken.

Decades later, Meena found herself back on the train to Rameswaram, this time with her grandchildren. The familiar sights and sounds of the station brought a wave of nostalgia, and as the train chugged along the tracks, she gazed out of the window, lost in thought. Her grandchildren played nearby, their laughter echoing the compartment, but her mind was far away, reliving that unforgettable journey.

At Rameswaram, while her family explored the temple, Meena stayed behind, sitting on a bench near the station. She watched the trains coming and going, her heart heavy with bittersweet memories. She knew she would never see him again, but the hope she carried all those years endured, a testament to the power of fleeting connections.

The Waiting

The old man stood alone at the bus stop, his frail body leaning heavily against the weathered post. His frame, hunched and worn from years of relentless labour, seemed on the verge of collapsing under the weight of existence. His skin, paper-thin and mottled with the marks of time, stretched taut over his gaunt frame. He wore a tattered square of cloth draped over his shoulders, its frayed edges fluttering in the cool evening breeze. The fabric, once vibrant, had faded to a lifeless hue, much like the life it covered.

For years, he had worked at the factory, a place where time blurred into a perpetual cycle of noise and toil. The relentless clanging of machines still echoed in his ears, a backdrop to a life devoid of relief. Days bled into nights without distinction, and the concept of time had long since lost its meaning. But tonight was different. Tonight, he clung to the fragile hope of escape. It was the eve of a festival, and after three gruelling shifts, he was finally going home.

Home—a modest, crumbling house at the edge of the village. It wasn't much, but it was his sanctuary. There, the silence was softer, punctuated by the rustling of leaves and the occasional murmur of distant voices. It was a place where he could shed the burdens of his existence, if only for a few fleeting hours. He longed for the familiar embrace of his worn-out cot, where he could collapse and let the world fade away.

The bus stop stood empty, the streetlights casting long, solitary shadows that stretched across the cracked pavement. The old man waited, his tired eyes fixed on the distance. Every so often, a faint light would appear far down the road, and his heart would leap with hope. Straightening his weary frame, he would squint into the darkness, only to watch the light draw closer and reveal itself as a car. The cars sped past him without pausing, their occupants oblivious to the solitary figure standing in the shadows. Each time, the weight of disappointment pressed heavier on his sagging shoulders.

Yet, he waited. What choice did he have? The factory had taken everything from him—his strength, his youth, even his sense of time. All that remained was hope, fragile and wavering. The hope that the bus would come and carry him away from this endless cycle of labour and waiting.

Minutes or perhaps hours passed—he couldn't tell. The road stayed silent, except for the occasional roar of a passing car. The chill of the night deepened, the wind cutting through his thin clothes like a blade. He shivered, his body trembling with the cold, but he remained rooted to the spot. There was no one else at the bus stop, no one to tell him to go home, no one to care whether he made it back or not. He was alone, just as he had always been.

The distant hum of a car radio drifted through the air, its crackling voice barely audible. It spoke of a bus strike, the drivers demanding better pay and the government refusing to negotiate. The strike had been ongoing for days, and it seemed no resolution was in sight. The words floated past the old man, barely registering in his tired mind. He didn't understand why the bus was late, nor did he comprehend the reasons behind the strike. All he knew was that he had to wait—because waiting was all he had left.

The night stretched on, and the old man's exhaustion deepened. His legs ached, his back throbbed, and his eyelids grew heavy. Yet, he refused to leave. The thought of returning to the factory or spending another night in its cold, unforgiving dormitory was unbearable. Home was his only refuge, the only place where he could feel human, even if just for a night.

As the first light of dawn began to creep over the horizon, painting the sky in hues of pink and orange, the old man's strength finally gave out. His knees buckled, and he slid down the post, his body crumpling to the ground like a puppet with its strings cut. He leaned against the post, his eyes closing as fatigue overtook him. The road stretched out before him, empty and silent, a metaphor for the life he had lived.

He sat there, waiting, even as the world around him began to stir. Commuters passed by, their hurried footsteps echoing against the pavement. A young couple, arm in arm, cast a fleeting glance at the old man before continuing on their way. A street vendor set up his cart nearby, the aroma of freshly brewed tea wafting through the air. Life moved on, indifferent to the solitary figure who had once waited with hope but now waited with nothing at all.

The hours slipped by, and the old man remained motionless, his breathing shallow and his gaze unfocused. A group of children on their way to school paused to look at him, their curious whispers cutting through the morning air. One of them approached cautiously, her small hand reaching out to shake his shoulder. 'Thaatha, are you okay?' she asked, her voice trembling with concern.

The old man stirred slightly, his eyelids fluttering open. He looked at the girl, his expression blank, as if struggling to recall where he was or why he was there. 'I'm waiting for the bus,' he mumbled, his voice barely audible.

The girl's brow furrowed in confusion. 'But there's no bus today. Didn't you hear? The drivers are on strike.'

Her words lingered in the air, a harsh confirmation of the old man's fears. He nodded faintly, a faint smile crept onto his lips. 'It's okay,' he whispered. 'I'll keep waiting.'

The children exchanged uneasy glances before being called away by their teacher, who ushered them along with a wave. The old man watched them go, their laughter fading into the distance. He leaned his head back against the post, his eyes closing once more. The warmth of the morning sun bathed his face, a small comfort in an otherwise cold and unyielding world.

As the day wore on, the old man's figure became a fixture of the bus stop, a silent symbol of endurance and despair. Passersby noticed him but said nothing, their lives too occupied to spare even a fleeting thought for the stranger who waited for a bus that would never come. And so, he remained, waiting, as the steady rhythm of life continued around him.

A Love Left Behind

Ananya sat in front of the mirror, her fingers fumbling with the delicate gold necklace around her neck. The soft light of the setting sun filtered through the curtains, casting a warm glow over her face. Today marked five years since she had married Vikram. It was supposed to be a joyous milestone, a celebration of love and togetherness. Yet, as she stared at her reflection, a profound emptiness settled in her chest. The woman looking back at her was a stranger—someone who had given too much of herself and received too little in return.

Her phone rang, breaking the heavy silence in the room. Ananya's heart quickened as Vikram's name flashed on the screen. She picked up, hoping against hope for some sweetness in his tone, some words that might bridge the growing emotional chasm between them.

'Happy anniversary,' Vikram said, his voice polite but devoid of warmth. 'Can you believe it's been five years? Look at us, how far we've come.'

'Yes, it's been five years,' Ananya replied, forcing a smile though he couldn't see it. She waited, clinging to the faint hope that he might say something more meaningful. But instead, Vikram's tone turned practical, hurried.

'I've got a meeting in a few minutes. I'll call you later,' he said before ending the call, leaving her holding the phone, her heart sinking further into the void.

Moments later, her phone rang again. This time, when she glanced at the screen, her breath caught. It was Arjun. Her fingers hesitated over the screen before she answered.

'Happy anniversary, my dear wife,' came Arjun's voice, warm and full of affection. Like a calming tide washing over jagged rocks, his words softened the pain within her, wrapping around her like a comforting embrace.

'Thank you, Arjun,' she whispered, her voice trembling with emotion. His simple words carried the depth and love she so desperately craved.

After a few tender exchanges, the call ended. But as the screen went dark, the weight of her reality came crashing back. The love she sought was fleeting, scattered between moments with two men who seemed incapable of truly seeing her. Vikram, her husband, offered her stability but no warmth, while Arjun, the man she had once believed to be her saviour, had shown her the darker sides of love.

Ananya's relationship with Arjun had always been complicated. When she first met him, he had seemed like everything Vikram wasn't— charming, passionate, and full of life. He had been her mentor, her guide, and for a while, her anchor. She had fallen hard and fast, believing he understood her in ways no one else ever could. But as time went on, she began to see the cracks.

Arjun's confidence, which had initially drawn her to him, now felt suffocatingly self-centred. He dismissed her ideas during their creative collaborations, subtly undermining her confidence. 'You're too emotional,' he would say. 'You let your feelings cloud your judgment.'

His control reached beyond their work. Gradually, Arjun began isolating her, discouraging her from meeting friends or maintaining relationships outside of their world. 'They're not good for you,' he would insist. 'You don't need anyone else. I'm all you need.'

Ananya, yearning for love and approval, let it happen. She convinced herself that Arjun knew best , that his actions were born out of care. But deep down, she missed the freedom of her old life—the spontaneous laughter, the late-night conversations with friends, the joy of simply being herself.

One evening, after watching a movie together, Ananya felt a wave of loneliness wash over her. She had been feeling off all day—tired, emotional, and in desperate need of connection. As they walked out of the theatre, she turned to Arjun, her voice soft and hesitant. 'Can I stay with you tonight? I don't want to be alone.'

Arjun paused, his hand on the car door. He didn't look at her. 'You should go home and sleep, Ananya,' he said flatly, avoiding her gaze. His words, so dismissive, felt like a slap in the face.

The ride back was silent, the weight of unspoken emotions filling the car. When they reached her apartment, Arjun didn't even look at her as she stepped out. 'Goodnight,' he said, his tone cold and distant. Ananya stood on the curb, watching his car disappear into the night, her heart heavy with unspoken words.

Later that night, as she lay staring at the ceiling, her phone rang. It was Arjun. 'Where are you?' he asked, his voice casual, as though nothing had happened.

Ananya's frustration boiled over. 'Why do you even care?' she snapped, unable to hide the hurt in her voice. 'You didn't care when I needed you earlier.'

'What's wrong with you?' Arjun asked, clearly taken back. 'Why are you talking like this?'

Ananya's emotions, which she had been holding back all evening, burst forth. 'I wanted to be with you tonight, Arjun. I didn't want to be alone.

But you didn't even care. You just told me to go home and sleep like it was nothing.'

There was a long pause on the other end of the line before Arjun spoke, his voice tinged with frustration. 'Ananya, what if I was admitted to the hospital tonight? What would you have done? Would you still fight with me like this if I was in the hospital?'

'It's not about that, Arjun!' she cried, her voice breaking. 'It's about tonight, about how I needed you and you weren't there. That's why I wanted a relationship, for moments like these when I need someone to just be there for me. But you didn't feel that. Instead, you're blaming me for wanting you, for needing you.'

Arjun sighed, his tone growing colder. 'You have to understand, Ananya, I'm a Familiar person. I can't just go around or stay whenever you want. I can't be there all the time. You have to be more understanding.' The dismissiveness in his voice pushed her over the edge. 'I don't want a relationship like this, Arjun,' she said, her voice trembling with anger and sadness. 'I don't want to feel like I'm asking for too much just because I… I want to be with the person I love.'

There was a sharp intake of breath from Arjun. When he spoke again, his voice was icy. 'Then maybe you don't deserve a person like me, Ananya.'

The words hit her like a slap in the face. All the love, all the longing she had felt for him crumbled under the weight of his callousness. 'Maybe I don't,' she whispered, her voice choking with tears.

The call ended abruptly, leaving Ananya staring at the phone in disbelief. The man who had once made her feel cherished now made her feel small, unworthy. She could no longer hold back the tears. They flowed freely, her sobs echoing in the emptiness of her room.

She spent the night crying, her heart breaking with every minute that passed. In her despair, she sent him message after message, hoping for some response, some sign that he cared. But when he finally came online, he didn't bother to react. He simply went offline, leaving her messages unread, her pain unacknowledged.

Ananya felt utterly alone, broken into pieces. The man she had believed she loved, the man for whom she had sacrificed so much, had shown her his true colours. He was self-centred, more concerned with his image and convenience than with her feelings. And now, he had left her to pick up the shattered remains of her heart.

The morning after the argument was one of the hardest Ananya had ever faced. She woke with swollen eyes, her body exhausted from a night of tears. The emotional weight of the previous night pressed down on her, but amid the pain, there was a small spark of determination. She knew she couldn't continue living this way—dependent on someone who couldn't truly love or support her.

Ananya took a deep breath and made a decision: she would rebuild herself, piece by piece, from the ashes of her broken heart. She started small, focusing on the things that once brought her joy but had been overshadowed by her relationship with Arjun.

She immersed herself in writing, but this time, it was different. She wrote not to impress or to gain approval—but for herself. Her stories turned into a form of therapy, a way to process the emotions she had bottled up for so long. The words flowed more freely than they ever had, filled with the raw honesty of her experiences.

But writing wasn't enough. Ananya knew she needed to reconnect with the world she had isolated herself from. She reached out to old friends, people she had pushed away at Arjun's insistence. To her relief, many of them welcomed her back with open arms, understanding and supportive. Slowly, she began to rebuild her social circle, surrounding herself with people who valued her for who she was, not for what they expected her to be.

Ananya also started taking better care of herself, both physically and mentally. She began a morning routine of meditation and journaling, helping her to centre herself before the day began. She joined a yoga class, finding peace in the movements and the collective energy of others who, like her, were seeking balance in their lives.

As the weeks turned into months, Ananya felt the heavy weight of her past lift, little by little. She was still healing—there were days when the memories of Arjun's words would creep back in, threatening to pull her down. But each time, she reminded herself of how far she had come, of the strength she had found within herself.

Ananya's life transformed in ways she never imagined. She was no longer the woman who sought validation from others, who had depended on a man to make her feel loved. She had found that love within herself, and it had made her stronger than ever.

Her travels healed her and brought unexpected success. Her writings, deeply inspired by the places she'd seen and the people she'd met, began to gain recognition. Publishers took notice, and soon, her stories were being shared with a wide audience. Ananya's journey of healing and self-discovery resonated with many, her words touching hearts and inspiring others to find their own strength.

Yet, even in her newfound success, there were moments when memories of Arjun surfaced. She would occasionally wonder how he was, but these thoughts no longer had the power to stir pain or longing. She had moved on, having reclaimed her life and her happiness.

Months later, Ananya found herself standing at the front of a crowded bookstore, signing copies of her newly published book. The event was more than just a celebration of her success—it was a testament to her journey, to the strength she had found within herself. As she greeted each reader, she felt a deep sense of fulfilment. This was her life now, and it was one she had built on her terms.

As the event drew to a close, she looked up and saw a familiar figure standing near the back of the store. It was Arjun. He approached her, a hesitant smile on his face, and for a moment, time seemed to stand still. 'I read your book,' he said quietly, his voice holding a mix of admiration and something else—perhaps regret. 'It's... powerful. You've come a long way.'

Ananya smiled, but it was a smile of peace, not of longing. She no longer needed anything from him—no validation, no apology. 'Thank you, Arjun,' she replied with warm yet calm detachment. 'I have.'

They exchanged a few more words, but the conversation was brief, almost anticlimactic. As Arjun walked away, Ananya felt nothing but a deep sense of closure. The man who was once the centre of her world was now just a part of her past—a past she had learned from, but one she no longer needed to hold onto.

As the evening ended, Ananya walked out of the bookstore and into the city streets, feeling lighter than she had in years. The sun had set, but the city was alive with lights and movement, a reminder that life was always moving forward, just as she was.

She knew that her journey was far from over, but she also knew that whatever came next, she was ready for it. She had rebuilt herself from the ashes of her past, and now she stood tall, confident, and at peace with herself.

Her thoughts briefly drifted back to Arjun, but there was no more pain, no more longing. She had loved, she had lost, and she had found herself. And in the end, that was all she needed.

As Ananya walked into the night, she smiled, knowing that her story was just beginning—a story of strength, resilience, and the enduring power of self-love.

Whispers of the Night

Maya gripped the steering wheel tightly, her knuckles white against the leather. The engine's hum was the only sound accompanying her down the desolate, winding road. The headlights sliced through the darkness, illuminating a path that seemed as endless as the storm of thoughts swirling in her mind. On the surface, Maya's life appeared fine. She had a steady job, a comfortable apartment, and friends who seemed to care. But beneath it all was a void—an emptiness that gnawed at her ceaselessly, leaving her feeling adrift in a sea of doubt and despair.

This road was notorious, a stretch where many lives had been lost to accidents or, as the locals whispered, to the curse of unfulfilled dreams. Maya had heard these stories growing up, tales of how the road claimed those who had given up hope. Tonight, she found herself drawn to it, tempted by its promise of finality. If she was going to end it all, she reasoned, this would be the place—a poetic culmination to her restless, aimless journey.

The darkness outside mirrored the maze of her thoughts. Every failure, every rejection, every moment of loneliness played on repeat in her mind. It wasn't one event but an accumulation of tiny, crushing disappointments that had brought her here. Trust, once a natural part of her being, now felt like a foreign concept. She had pulled away from everyone she cared about, convinced that no one could truly understand her pain.

As the road stretched ahead, a figure emerged in the dim glow of her headlights. Maya's first instinct was to keep driving, but something made her slow down. The man stood at the roadside, his arm raised in a silent plea for help. He was older, perhaps in his late fifties, with silver hair and a calm disposition that contrasted sharply with the chaos within her.

Maya cautiously rolled down the window. 'Do you need a lift?' she asked, her voice quivering slightly.

The man smiled, a warm, calming smile that put her at ease. 'If it's not too much trouble,' he replied.

She unlocked the door, and he slid into the passenger seat. For a moment, they drove in silence, the rhythmic hum of the engine the only sound. Then, as if sensing her turmoil, he spoke.

'You know,' he began, his voice gentle and thoughtful, 'this road has seen many endings. But it's also witnessed many beginnings.'

Maya glanced at him, her curiosity piqued. 'Beginnings?'

He nodded, his gaze fixed on the road ahead. 'Yes. People come here lost and broken, thinking there's nothing left for them. But sometimes, when they least expect it, they find a reason to keep going.'

Maya let out a bitter laugh. 'I don't think I can find anything because all I lost is me.'

The man turned to her, his eyes kind and steady. 'You'd be surprised. Sometimes, we're so focused on what we've lost that we forget to look within ourselves. The answers are often closer than we think.'

She tightened her grip on the wheel. 'What if there's nothing left inside? What if you're just... empty?'

He smiled softly, a knowing smile that sent a shiver down her spine. 'You're not empty, Maya. You're just lost. And being lost doesn't mean you can't be found.'

Maya hesitated before whispering, 'But why do I feel this way? Like nothing matters?'

The man sighed, looking out at the winding road ahead. 'This is the problem with this generation,' he said. 'The world has changed. The competition has grown strong, and now, everyone is trying to prove themselves. Everyone is running in a race. In the process, we've lost the sense of connection with each other.'

Maya remained silent, absorbing his words.

'We have so much,' he continued, 'but we've forgotten the simple joys of life. We don't pause to feel, to connect, to just exist. The mere act of being human, of experiencing emotions, now feels like an unfamiliar thing to do. And that's why you feel empty—because you're trying to find meaning in achievements instead of in connection.'

Maya frowned. 'So what do I do? How do I fix this?'

He turned to her with a soft smile. 'Give love, Maya. Not to expect anything in return, but just to give. Find someone who feels like you do, someone who thinks the world is empty, and give them love. Maybe in doing so, you'll find yourself again.

Sometimes, when we help others find their light, we discover that we were never really lost.'

Her heart skipped a beat. She hadn't told him her name. She opened her mouth to question him but found herself unable to speak. Instead, she kept driving, the conversation unfolding in a way that felt both surreal and profoundly meaningful.

The man listened quietly as Maya poured out her fears and doubts. She spoke of the emptiness that consumed her, the way she felt disconnected from the world and from herself. He didn't interrupt or offer platitudes. He simply listened, his presence like a balm to her wounded soul.

As the car rounded a bend, the man began to speak of the road's history. 'This road has seen its share of tragedy,' he said, his voice heavy with emotion. 'But it's not the road that ends dreams. It's the choices we make.'

His words struck a chord deep within Maya. For the first time in months, a flicker of hope stirred within her—a tiny ember in the darkness of her despair. Maybe, she thought, there was a way forward. Maybe she didn't have to be defined by her pain.

They continued in silence for a while, the quiet hum of the engine filling the space between them. Eventually, the man asked her to stop at a crossroads. 'This is my stop,' he said, smiling gently as he reached for the door handle. Maya frowned, puzzled. The area was deserted, with no signs of life. 'Are you sure? There's nothing here.'

He nodded. 'I'm sure. Thank you, Maya. You've helped me more than you know.'

Before she could respond, he stepped out of the car and disappeared into the night. Maya sat there for a moment, trying to process everything that had just happened. She felt liberated, as though a heavy weight had finally been lifted. The thoughts of ending her life no longer held the same allure. Instead, she felt a quiet determination to face her challenges and find her way.

It wasn't until she started driving again that she noticed the small leather bag on the passenger seat. The man had left it behind. Her heart racing, she turned the car around and drove back to the crossroads, hoping to find him waiting for his bag.

But when she arrived, the road was empty. There was no sign of the man. Confused, she got out of the car, clutching the bag. That's when she saw it—a small, weathered tombstone beneath an old tree, almost hidden by the shadows. Her breath caught in her throat as she approached it, her eyes scanning the inscription:

'In memory of Vetri—Forever a traveller of the stars.'

Maya's knees buckled as the realization hit her. The man she had met wasn't just a stranger. He had died on this very road years ago, his body never found. His family had placed the memorial stone here, where his soul now roamed, helping lost travellers like her.

Tears welled up in her eyes as she stood before the tombstone, overwhelmed by a mix of emotions. Vetri had saved her, pulling her back from the edge of despair. The road that had taken so many dreams had, in the end, given her a new one.

With a trembling hand, Maya placed the bag by the tombstone, as if returning a piece of him to where it belonged. She whispered a quiet 'thank you' to the night, her voice carried away by the gentle breeze.

As she walked back to her car, the road ahead no longer seemed so daunting. It was still long, still winding, but she knew she could navigate it. Vetri's words echoed in her mind, a reminder that she wasn't empty, only lost—and now, she was found.

Winds of Change

Neha was born and raised in Mandya, a small district in Karnataka, known for its lush sugarcane fields and vibrant traditions. Her childhood was a mix of simple joys and quiet discontent. While the other girls in her village dreamt of marriage and a life centered around home and family, Neha's dreams reached far beyond the horizons of her small town. She was both a thinker and a dreamer.

After excelling in school, Neha moved to Mumbai, a city that offered her the freedom and opportunities she had yearned for. The bustling metropolis became her playground, a place where she carved out a space for herself as a marketing executive at a reputed firm. The city's chaos thrilled her, but as she entered her thirties, the weight of societal expectations began to press heavily on her. Her family, once proud of her ambition, began urging her to 'settle down.' Marriage proposals came and went, each more unsuitable than the last. Neha found herself unable to connect with men who seemed to embody the very traditions she had left behind.

She felt an insatiable frustration clawing at her thoughts. The pressures of her career, societal expectations, and her own restless spirit converged, leaving her yearning for clarity. On a whim, Neha decided to take a break—a journey to the mountains, where she hoped to find solace. Her trip would take her from the bustling plains of Punjab to the serene heights of Himachal Pradesh. She imagined the mountains, with their timeless serenity, might offer her the answers she sought.

Meanwhile, in Delhi, Saurabh was grappling with his own dissatisfaction. A successful IIM graduate working at a leading investment bank, his life was a whirlwind of high-stakes deals, late-night meetings, and unrelenting pressure. Though his career was the envy of many, Saurabh felt a gnawing emptiness. The corporate ladder he had climbed so rapidly had started to feel like a treadmill—each step forward brought him no closer to fulfilment.

In an effort to reconnect with inner self, Saurabh decided to escape the chaos of his life. He booked a solo retreat to Himachal Pradesh, intending to immerse himself in the mountains and find a semblance of balance.

Fate brought Neha and Saurabh together at a tea stall in Punjab, where they both waited for the same bus to Dharamshala. Saurabh was immediately struck by Neha's quiet confidence and the depth in her eyes. Neha, though preoccupied with her thoughts, couldn't help but notice Saurabh's calm attitude—a stark contrast to the hurried energy she often encountered in Mumbai.

Their journey began as strangers. When a massive traffic jam caused by an accident delayed the bus for hours, the passengers found themselves stranded. While many grew frustrated,

Saurabh saw it as an opportunity to help. He organised food and drinks for the elderly and scouted the area for makeshift toilets. His actions drew admiration from the passengers, including Neha, who watched with growing interest as he moved through the crowd with a calm and composed manner.

Their first conversation was sparked by a mutual frustration over the delay, but it quickly evolved into something deeper. They spoke about their careers, their dreams, and their frustrations. Saurabh was captivated by Neha's intellect and her thoughtful perspectives on life. Neha, in turn, was drawn to Saurabh's kindness and his ability to balance his corporate success with genuine compassion.

When the bus finally began moving again, they found themselves seated next to each other, their connection grew deeper with every mile. Upon arriving in Dharamshala, Saurabh suggested they explore the mountains together. What had initially been a solo retreat for both quickly became a shared journey.

Their days were filled with adventures—trekking through lush trails, discovering hidden waterfalls, and standing in awe of breathtaking vistas. Neha admired Saurabh's resilience as he traversed the rugged terrain with ease, while Saurabh was inspired by Neha's zest for life. Their nights were spent under a canopy of stars, sharing stories and dreams around a crackling campfire. They sang songs, some traditional, others playful and impromptu, their laughter echoing through the quiet wilderness.

One evening, they stumbled upon a local festival in a nearby village. The vibrant colours, rhythmic dances, and joyous energy were infectious. Neha joined in, her movements graceful and uninhibited, while Saurabh watched, mesmerised by her spirit.

They drank local wine, the warmth of the alcohol adding to the already intoxicating atmosphere. In those moments, they felt a freedom neither had experienced in years—a freedom from societal expectations, from professional pressures, and from their own self-imposed limitations.

As the days turned into weeks, Saurabh made a decision that surprised even himself—he extended his trip to spend more time with Neha. The connection they shared felt rare and precious, and he wasn't ready to let it go. Their bond deepened as they continued to explore the mountains, each day bringing new adventures and moments of vulnerability.

But all journeys must come to an end. On their final night together, as they sat by the campfire, Saurabh opened up about a secret he had been holding back. He disclosed that his family had already arranged his engagement, a commitment he felt obligated to honour. His words hung heavy in the air, and Neha felt her heart sink.

She had allowed herself to believe in the possibility of something more with Saurabh, but now she realised it wasn't meant to be. The pain was sharp, but as she looked at him, she understood his inner conflict. He cared deeply for her, but his sense of duty to his family was something he couldn't ignore.

At that moment, Neha made a choice. She could fight for what they had, or she could let go with grace. She chose the latter, understanding that while Saurabh had brought out the best in her, she didn't need him to complete her. The mountains taught her the importance of living in the moment, of embracing the beauty of fleeting connections.

The next morning, they parted ways with quiet understanding and mutual respect. Neha returned to Mumbai with a heart full of memories and a renewed sense of purpose. She realised that love wasn't about finding someone to fill the gaps in her life but about appreciating the moments of connection and growth along the way.

Saurabh also returned to Delhi, his time with Neha leaving a lasting mark on his soul. Though their paths diverged, the lessons they had learned from each other remained.

Neha carried the mountains within her—a reminder of the strength she had found and the freedom she had embraced. She no longer waited for Prince Charming to bring her happiness. Instead, she found joy in her own journey, knowing that she was enough.

Lucky, But Not Lucky

The streets lay quiet, bathed in the muted yellow glow of streetlights. A scrawny puppy curled up near a pile of trash, trembling in the cold. Its tiny frame was barely noticeable amidst the chaos of the bustling city. The puppy's breaths came in short, shallow puffs, and its ribs protruded sharply beneath its thin coat. Abandoned and hungry, it let out a faint whimper, a sound almost swallowed by the night.

Vinoth walked slowly along the street, his head low, his steps aimless. His clothes were tattered, his stomach empty, and his heart hollow. Life had not been kind to him. He had no family, no home, and no reason to keep going. Every day felt like a punishment, a relentless reminder of how little he had left.

As his gaze fell on the trembling puppy, something inside him shifted. The puppy flinched when Vinoth crouched beside it, but it didn't have the strength to run. He reached into his pocket and pulled out the only thing he had—a dry piece of bread he had saved for himself. He broke it into small pieces, gently placed them in front of the puppy. The little creature hesitated, its eyes wary, but hunger soon won over fear. It crept forward and began to eat, devouring the crumbs with desperate haste.

Vinoth watched in silence, his lips curving into a faint smile for the first time in what felt like years. 'Lucky,' he murmured, the word escaping him almost unconsciously. 'That's what I'll call you. Maybe you'll bring me some luck.'

But the truth was, Lucky wasn't just a name. It was a feeling. For the first time, something depended on Vinoth. This tiny, fragile creature gave him a purpose, a reason to get up each morning. Lucky was the only living being who had ever looked at him with trust, who had ever brought joy to his stray soul. Vinoth had never known that rescuing a helpless dog would change his life forever.

From that moment on, Vinoth and Lucky were inseparable. They wandered the streets together, sharing whatever scraps they could find, sleeping under bridges, and finding warmth in each other's company. Vinoth often spoke to Lucky as if the dog could understand every word. 'It's just you and me, buddy,' he would say, stroking Lucky's head. And Lucky, with his soulful eyes, would wag his tail in response, his trust in Vinoth absolute.

The world barely noticed them. They were just two forgotten lives, lost in the endless noise of the city. But to each other, they were everything.

One day, while searching for food, they stumbled upon a bustling film set. Bright lights illuminated the scene, and a cacophony of voices filled the air. Vinoth and Lucky stood at a distance, watching curiously. At the centre of the action was a sleek, well-trained dog performing tricks with ease. It leapt through hoops, barked on command, and carried out every trick flawlessly. The crowd clapped and cheered, and the trainer stood proudly beside the dog, basking in the glory.

Vinoth couldn't tear his eyes away. He watched as the trainer accepted a large payment from the director, his mind racing with possibilities. Could Lucky do that? Could they turn their lives around with a bit of training? The thought sparked hope in Vinoth. For the first time in years, hope flickered in his heart.

The idea obsessed him. Vinoth began training Lucky using whatever knowledge he could gather from observing trainers and imitating their methods. It wasn't easy. Lucky was clumsy at first, his movements awkward and uncertain. But he was eager to please, and his boundless energy kept Vinoth motivated. Slowly but surely, Lucky learned to follow commands, jump through hoops, and perform basic tricks. Their bond grew stronger with each day, rooted in trust and a shared will to survive.

Their hard work paid off when a small-time director noticed Lucky performing tricks in a park. Impressed by the dog's natural talent, he offered them a small role in his upcoming film. Vinoth couldn't believe it. They had gone from scrounging for scraps to stepping into the dazzling world of cinema.

Lucky's debut proved successful. Audiences fell in love with the scrappy dog with soulful eyes, and offers began pouring in. Vinoth and Lucky were no longer invisible. They were stars.

But fame has a way of changing people. The money and attention transformed Vinoth. What had started as a relationship built on love and trust slowly turned into one driven by ambition. Vinoth became obsessed with making Lucky the biggest star in the industry. He pushed the dog harder, demanding perfection with every performance. When Lucky faltered, Vinoth's patience wore thin. He began using harsher methods—electric shocks to enforce commands, long hours of gruelling training, and withholding food as punishment.

Lucky's life, once filled with freedom and love, became a never-ending cycle of stunts and exhaustion. The dog's spirit began to break. The bond that had once been their lifeline now felt like a chain, binding Lucky to a life of servitude.

As Lucky's fame grew, so did Vinoth's desperation for more. Film after film, commercial after commercial, Lucky's name became a brand. Fans clamoured for photos, directors demanded his presence, and his face adorned billboards across the city. But behind the glamour was a dog who had lost everything that once made life worth living. Lucky longed for the days when his world was just Vinoth and the streets. At least then, he had been free.

Today was no different. The set hummed with energy as cameras rolled and instructions echoed. Lucky stood silently, his body weak from hunger and fatigue. Vinoth barked commands, his tone sharp and impatient. 'One more, Lucky,' he muttered. 'Just one more.'

The stunt carried real danger. Lucky had to leap from a high platform into a pool of water below. The crowd watched eagerly, unaware of the toll the years had taken on the once-vibrant dog. Lucky looked down at the platform, then up at the sky. Memories flooded his mind—the day Vinoth had found him, the warmth of their early days, the love that had once defined their lives. For a brief moment, the noise of the set faded, leaving only silence.

With a deep breath, Lucky leapt. For the first time in years, he felt weightless. Free. The wind whistled past his ears, the world a blur around him. Lucky wasn't thinking about where he would land. He wasn't thinking about the applause or the cameras waiting below. All that mattered was the leap—the one moment he chose freedom over fear.

Because every ending is a new beginning. And for Lucky, this was the start of something new.

The Last Splash

The house smelled of camphor and stale incense. In the middle of the hall, wrapped in a white veshti and covered in sandalwood paste and flowers, lay Krishnamoorthy. People surrounded him—some weeping, some murmuring prayers, some just watching. Everyone had something to say, someone to console, some memory to recall.

Ponnumani sat in the corner, still and silent.

There was no trace of grief on her face. Only calm. But not the kind born of peace. It was the calm that comes after years of exhaustion—after crying every night for so long that your tears simply dry out.

She hadn't always been this way.

Ponnumani was born in Singampunari, a small village near Karaikudi. Her mother worked as a house-help in a wealthy Chettiyar household. Her father died when she was young, and since then, her mother did everything she could to raise her 'right.' No education, no dreams—just duties. Her mother believed a girl's life began and ended in her husband's shadow.

She repeated the same line to Ponnumani every night: *'Be a good wife. That's enough. That's what we're meant to be.'*

Ponnumani believed her.

She was in her early twenties when she first met Krishnamoorthy. He worked temporarily as the driver for the Chettiyar family, visiting from another town. One afternoon, he asked for water, and she, shy and soft-spoken, gave it to him without a word. That tiny moment, that innocent act, became her downfall.

People in the village began to talk. Rumours spread like wildfire—whispers that they had something going on. That she was no longer 'pure.' And to silence the tongues, her mother agreed to the only 'honourable' solution: marriage.

Ponnumani didn't protest. She thought maybe this was fate. Perhaps marriage would give her a life better than her mother's.

But hope was short-lived.

After their marriage, they moved to Trichy for better job opportunities. Krishnamoorthy tried different driving jobs, but none lasted more than a few months. He had a weakness—alcohol. He'd drink during duty, lose his temper, miss workdays. Slowly, he became known for his habit rather than his skill.

Ponnumani took up work as a helper in a nearby school—an *aya amma*, cleaning toilets, wiping floors, serving lunch to noisy children. The pay was meagre, but it kept her going.

Somewhere along the way, she found a small puppy abandoned in the street. She took him in, fed him scraps, named him Raju. He became her child, the only creature in the world that looked at her with unconditional love.

One day, after saving small coins for weeks, she decided to buy him a little treat—some meat from the butcher. But

Krishnamoorthy saw the money and took it, promising to return. He didn't. That night, he came home drunk, and Raju went to bed hungry. Ponnumani never said a word. She just held the pup close and cried in the dark.

Then came the worst day of her life.

A neighbour brought the news—her mother had passed away in Singampunari. Ponnumani was the only daughter, the only one left to perform the rituals. She panicked, uncertain of what to do. She asked Krishnamoorthy to get the basic items for her trip—camphor, rice, some coins, and a bus ticket. He nodded, told her to wait. But he never returned that night.

The next morning, she went alone. Her mother's body lay in the house, decaying in the summer heat, waiting for her arrival. Ponnumani stood over the body, numb with guilt—not just for being late, but for believing that somehow, her husband would come through.

Yet, she still didn't leave him.

Why?

Because he wasn't evil. He wasn't violent. He didn't hit her or scream. He just *didn't care enough*. And she? She didn't know any better. She didn't know where else to go.

By the time doctors said he had liver cirrhosis, it was too late. They told him to stop drinking. He nodded politely, then walked to the nearest shop and bought a quarter bottle.

And now, here he was. Cold. Still. And finally, resting.

Ponnumani stood up quietly while everyone was preparing for the rituals. One of the steps was to remove her **mangalsutra**—the symbol of her bondage. But before that, she walked into the back bathroom. The mirror was foggy, the walls were cracked, and she stared at her reflection.

She hadn't looked at herself properly in years.

Her sindoor. Her bangles. Her thali. The flowers in her hair. All the things that told the world she belonged to someone. That she was his.

From tomorrow, none of this will be there.

But something else would finally arrive—**peace**.

She cupped water in her hands and splashed her face. Once. Twice. She didn't cry. Not because she was in shock, as the relatives whispered, but because she had *run out of tears*—she had cried them all over the last fifteen years.

When she returned to the hall, people glanced at with pity. 'Poor thing,' someone said. 'She's too shocked to cry.' Another said, 'No matter how much he drank, he always came home to her.'

Yes, he did come home. And that arrival—every single time—was her nightmare.

Today, for the first time, **he wouldn't come back**. And that was the most peaceful thought she'd had in years.

They took the body, and the men carried it through the streets, chanting, followed by relatives wailing loudly. Ponnumani didn't follow. She sat on the doorstep, staring at the road, her eyes blank, her mind was still.

That night she didn't sleep.

She sat by the door, eyes fixed on the entrance—out of habit. Waiting. Even though there was no one to wait for anymore.

In the morning, the house was filled with voices again. People cleaning, rearranging things, preparing meals. A cousin threw a bucket of water into the front yard to wash away the leftover ash. Some of it splashed on Ponnumani's face.

She blinked—suddenly alert, as if waking from a long, long dream.

She stood up, tied her hair, picked up her old basket, poured water into a brass tumbler, sipped it slowly, and walked out the door.

She didn't look back.

She had a school to get to.

Tracks and Tales: Stories of Women, Journeys, and Hope by Priya Rajendran

Amid the hum of trains, waiting at bus stops, the quiet of village courtyards, and the chaos of city streets—every life carries a story. *Tracks and Tales* presents together sixteen soulful narratives from everyday India, where resilience meets vulnerability, and hope emerges from the most unlikeliest corners.

From an elderly woman boarding her first train alone to a young girl rediscovering strength in loss, these stories don't promise fairy tale endings—they reflect raw truth. Raw, tender, and often unspoken, these are tales of people you pass by every day—each carrying a world within.

Tracks and Tales takes you on a journey of emotions, inviting you to pause, reflect, and feel.

Glossary

Pattupaavadai – Traditional silk skirt and blouse worn by young girls

Anni – Sister-in-law (elder brother's wife)

Kannadi Valayal – Glass bangles (A traditional circular ornament made of colored glass, worn around the wrist, commonly seen in Indian culture as a symbol of femininity, festivity, or marital status.)

Marumagaley – Daughter-in-law (Literally means *daughter-in-law* in Tamil. Traditionally used for a son's wife, but in colloquial usage, it is also used as a term of endearment for a brother's daughter or a young woman in the family.)

Mookambika Devi – A revered Hindu goddess, worshipped in Kollur, Karnataka

Paati – Grandmother

Theni – A district in Tamil Nadu, known for its agriculture and scenic beauty

Tiruvannamalai – A district in Tamil Nadu, also a spiritual destination

Madurai – A major city in Tamil Nadu, known for its rich culture and ancient temples

Pudukottai – A district in Tamil Nadu

Alangudi – A small town in Pudukottai district

Inja – A colloquial, affectionate term used in parts of southern Tamil Nadu (often by men for their wives or beloved ones)

Appa – Father

Coimbatore/Ooty – Cities in Tamil Nadu; Ooty is a hill station, Coimbatore is a major city

Megamazhai – name of a remote Tamil village

Alagar Kovil – A sacred temple near Madurai

Suruli Falls – A popular waterfall in Tamil Nadu

Pamban Bridge – A historic railway bridge connecting Rameswaram to mainland India

Thali – A sacred necklace tied by the groom around the bride's neck during Hindu weddings; symbol of marriage

Veshti – Traditional South Indian white garment worn by men, especially during rituals

Chettiyar – A traditionally wealthy mercantile and banking community in Tamil Nadu

Rasam – ரசம் A tangy, peppery South Indian soup often served with rice

Singampunari – A town in Tamil Nadu

Karaikudi – A prominent town in Tamil Nadu, known for Chettinad culture and architecture

Trichy – Short for Tiruchirapalli, a major city in Tamil Nadu

Ayya – A respectful way of addressing an elderly man

Pongal – A traditional harvest festival celebrated in Tamil Nadu

Thuni – Clothes; sometimes used colloquially in rural storytelling

IndiePress

The best route your story can take.

To publish your own book, contact us.

We publish poetry collections, short story collections, novellas and novels.

contact@http://indiepress.in/

Instagram- indie_press